ISBN 0-590-44559-6

Text copyright © 1992 by Roberta Rauch.
Illustrations copyright © 1992 by Leonard Weisgard.
All rights reserved. Published by Scholastic Inc.
BLUE RIBBON is a registered trademark of Scholastic Inc.

12 11 10 9 8 7 6 5 4 3 2 1   8   4 5 6 7 8 9/9

Printed in the U.S.A.   08

Book design by Laurie McBarnette

The artwork for this book was done in mixed media technique including the use of casein, watercolor, crayon, and ink.

RED LIGHT, GREEN LIGHT

Written by Margaret Wise Brown

Illustrated by Leonard Weisgard

SCHOLASTIC INC.

New York   Toronto   London   Auckland   Sydney

RED LIGHT

GREEN LIGHT

GOOD MORNING

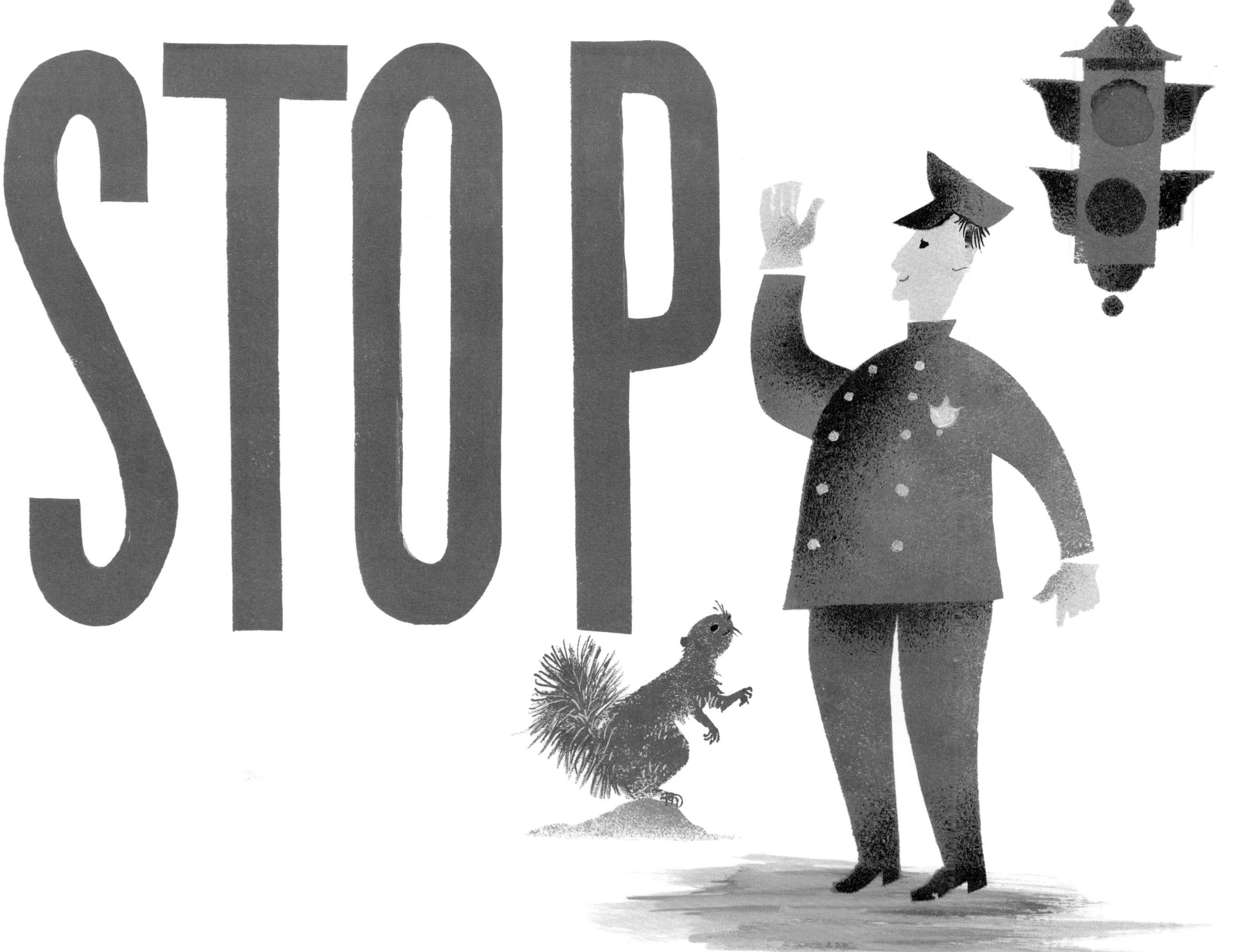
STOP

In the morning they all came out of their houses.

Red Light they can't go.

Green Light they can go.

The truck came out of the truck's house

a garage.

The car came out of the car's house

another garage.

The jeep came out of the jeep's house

a tent.

The horse came out of the horse's house

The boy came out of the boy's house

a *home*.

The dog came out of the dog's house

a *kennel*.

The cat climbed down from the cat's house

a *tree*.

(This was a wild cat.)

And the mouse came out of the house of the mouse

a *hole*.

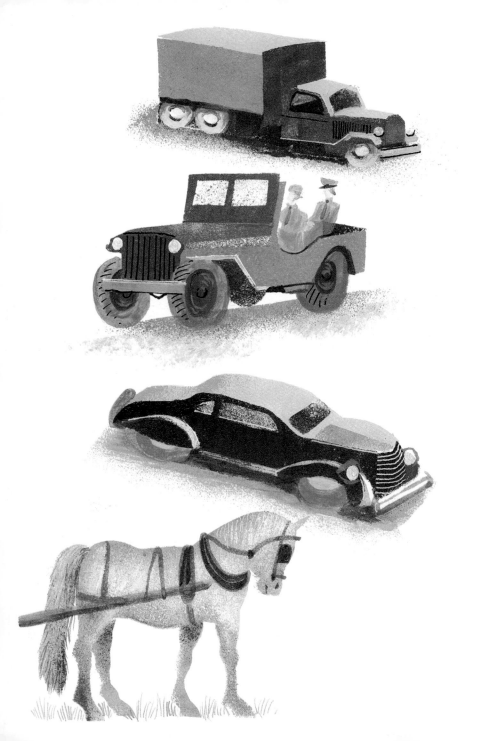

Red Light they can't go.

Green Light they can.

And they all went down
their own roads.
Truck and car and bicycle
and horse roads
Jeep roads across fields

Dog roads

Cat roads

And mouse roads through the grass.

Green Light they can go.

Red Light they can't.

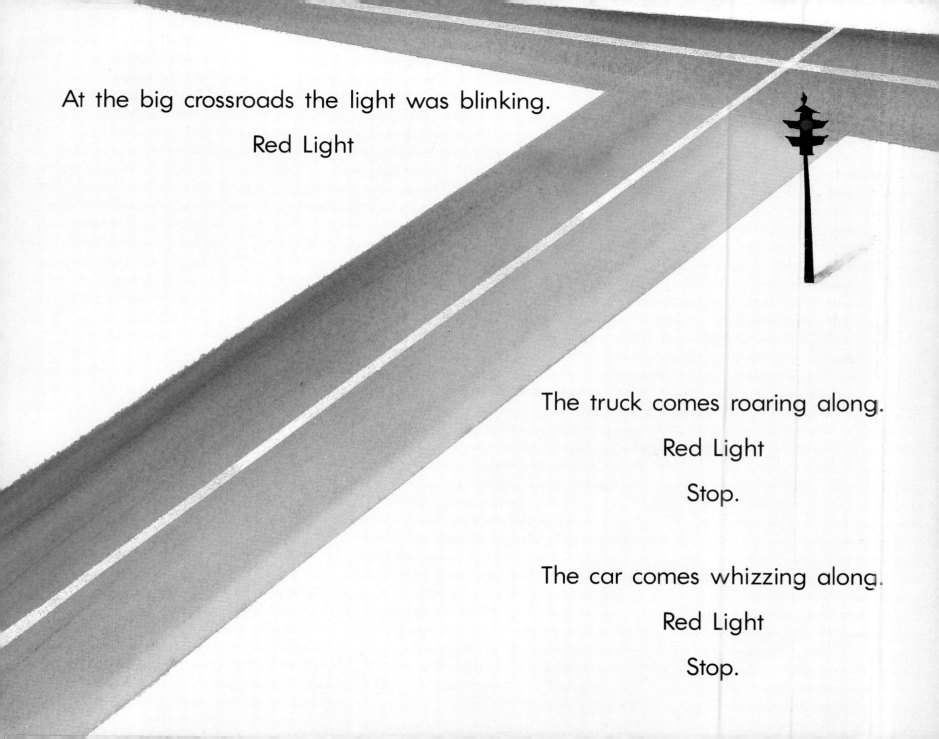

At the big crossroads the light was blinking.

Red Light

The truck comes roaring along.

Red Light

Stop.

The car comes whizzing along.

Red Light

Stop.

The jeep comes jeeping along.

Red Light

Stop.

The horse comes trotting along.

Red Light

Stop.

The cat comes creeping along.

Red Light

Stop.

RED LIGHT

The mouse came along.

Red Light a bunny's eyes.

Green Light a cat's.

STOP

GREEN LIGHT

Green Light they did go.

Red Light they didn't.

They went around all day until it was night.

Then all the lights turned on along the
roads and in the houses because it was night.
And they all went home.

Red Light they didn't go.
Green Light they did.

The truck went into the truck's house

a garage.

The car went into the car's house

another garage.

The jeep went into the jeep's house

a tent.

The horse went into the horse's house

a barn.

The boy went into the boy's house

a *home*.

The dog went into the dog's house

a *kennel*.

The cat went into the cat's house

a *tree*.

(This was a wild cat.)

And the mouse crept into the house of the mouse

a *hole*.

Red Light they can't go.

Green Light they can.

All things were asleep.

Through holes and doors and windows
lights blinked off
until there was only a Red Light
and a Green Light
blinking in the darkness.

RED LIGHT

GREEN LIGHT

GOOD NIGHT

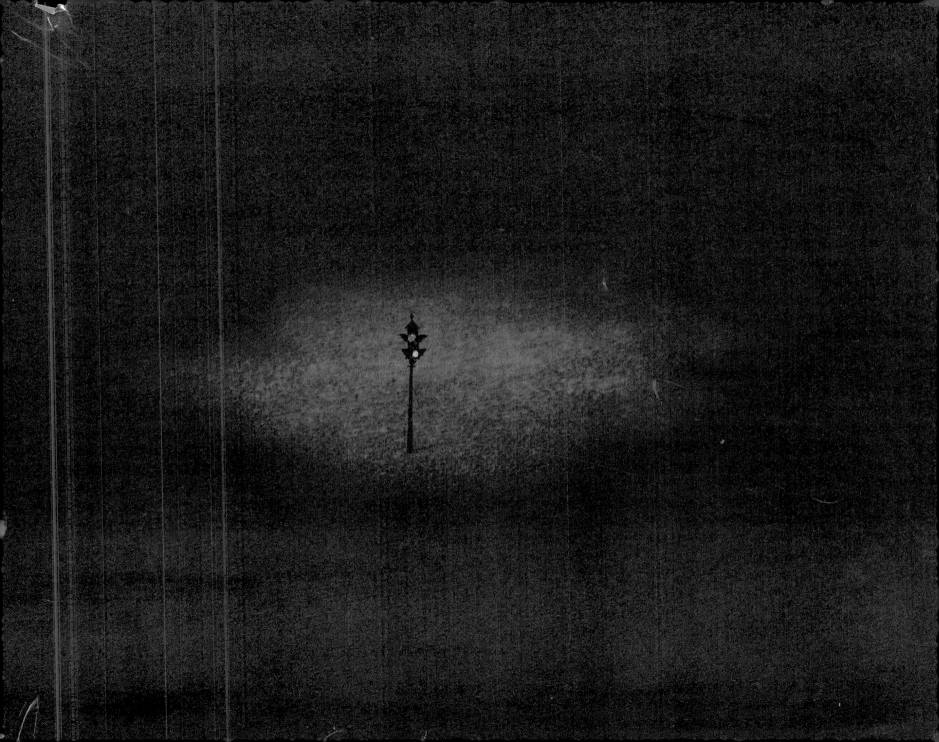